For:

_____

Library of Congress Cataloging-in-Publication Data available.

ISBN 978-1-7972-1007-0

Manufactured in China.

MIX
Paper from
responsible sources
FSC™ C104723

Design by Lydia Ortiz and Abbie Goveia.
Typeset in Zemke Hand.
The illustrations in this book were rendered in mixed media.

10 9 8 7 6 5 4 3 2 1

Chronicle Books LLC
680 Second Street
San Francisco, California 94107

Chronicle Books—we see things differently.
Become part of our community at www.chroniclekids.com.

I
LOVE
YOU
LIKE

Lisa Swerling
&
Ralph Lazar

chronicle books·san francisco

I love you like
a cuddle
loves

a bunny,

like a bear
loves

honey,

and like a clown
loves . . .

funny!

I love you like a slope
loves . . .

a sled,

like a hat
loves

a head,

and like "sleepy"
loves

a bed.

I love you like
a shepherd loves

his flock,

like a boat
loves

a dock,

and like a foot
loves

a sock.

I love you like a ball
loves

a game,

like a singer
loves . . .

fame,

and like
a candle
loves

a flame.

I love you like
a party
loves

a cake,

like a canoe
loves . . .

a lake,

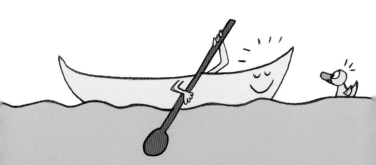

and like a gardener
loves

a rake.

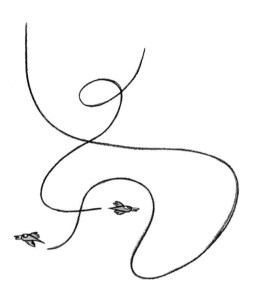

I love you like
a pilot loves

a plane,

like Tarzan
loves

Jane,

and like
a flower
loves . . .

the rain.

I love you like
a cat loves

the sun,

like kids love

fun,

and like
a puppy
loves

to run.

I love you like
a pirate
loves

an X,

like a witch
loves

a hex,

and like
a muscle
loves

to flex.

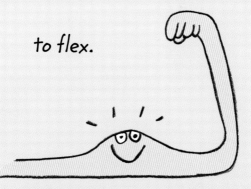

I love you like
a spout loves

a whale,

like a shell
loves

a snail,

and like a wag
loves

a tail.

like Beauty
loves

the Beast,

and like a table
loves

a feast.

I love you like
pizza loves . . .

cheese,

like a sailor
loves . . .

a breeze,

and like
a lemon loves

a squeeze.

I love you like
a baguette

loves France,

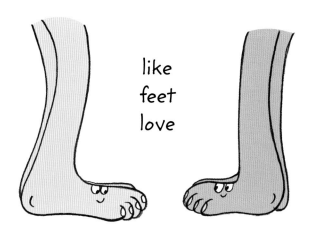

like
feet
love

to dance,

and like a heart loves

romance.

Although these pairings
are all true,
sometimes simpler
words will do. . . .

To put it plainly . . .

I LOVE YOU!

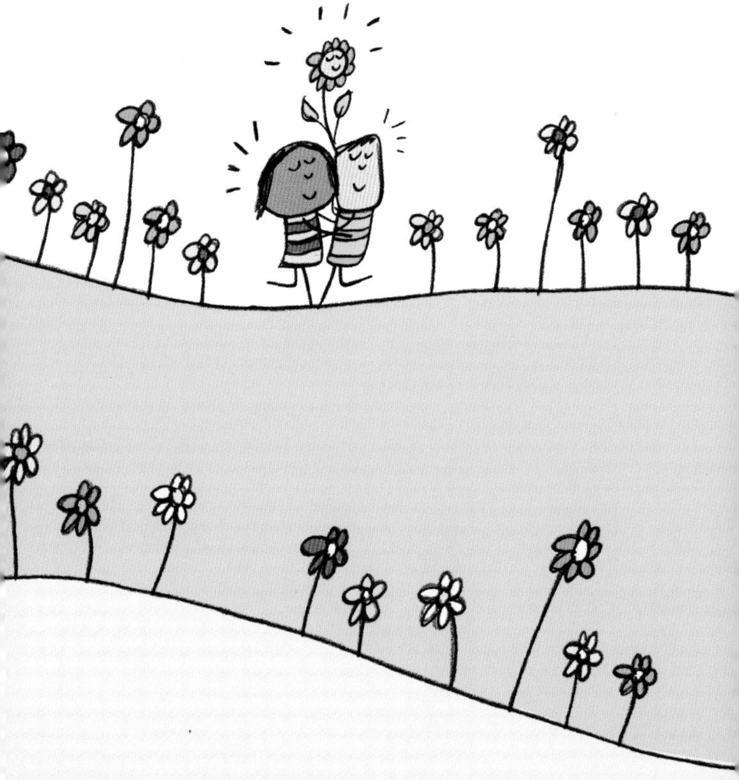